This edition published by Parragon in 2009

Parragon
Queen Street House
4 Queen Street
Bath BA1 1HE, UK

Copyright © Parragon Books Ltd 2008

ISBN 978-1-4075-8366-2
Printed in China

PrinceSS
stories

Bath New York Singapore Hong Kong Cologne Delhi Melbourne

Two Princesses

Once upon a time, a long time ago, there lived twin princesses called Charmina and Charlotte.

Even though they were twins, they were opposites. Princess Charmina always curtsied politely to the king and queen. And she stood very still while the dressmakers came to fit her new ball gown. Princess Charlotte was very different!

"Why do I have to dress like a puffball?" grumbled Princess Charlotte when it was her turn to have a new ball gown fitted.

"How dare you speak to us like that!" her parents cried.

But she did dare. She dared to run barefoot through the gardens. She dared to wear her shabbiest clothes. In fact, she didn't behave like a princess at all!

One day there was to be a ball at the palace. The guests of honor were two princes from the next kingdom.

"Why don't you go for a walk until our guests arrive?" suggested the queen to the two princesses, who were already dressed. "But stay together, don't get dirty, and don't be late!"

The princesses walked to the bottom of the palace gardens. "Let's go into the forest," said Princess Charlotte.

"I don't think we should," said Princess Charmina. "Our gowns will get dirty." But Princess Charlotte had already set off.

They hadn't gone far when they heard a strange noise

coming from the next clearing.

"Let's turn back!" said Princess Charmina.

"It might be someone in distress!" said Princess Charlotte. "We have to check!"

They peeked round a tree into the clearing. There were two horses, but there was no sign of their riders.

Then a voice called out, "Who's there?"

"Look!" said Princess Charmina. In the middle of the clearing there was a deep pit. The princesses crept up to it and peered over the edge. Princess Charmina stared in astonishment. Princess Charlotte burst out laughing. There at the bottom of the pit were the two princes.

"Well, don't just stand there," said the princes. "Get some rope from our saddlebags and help us out!"

The two princesses threw a rope down to the princes and tied the other end to the horses. Soon the princes were rescued.

Everyone enjoyed the ball that evening. The two princesses and two princes danced all night. And from that time on, Charlotte paid more attention to her gowns and hair, while Charmina became a little more playful and daring!

Fairer Princess Sarah

Sarah was the fairest royal princess in the land,
And every prince for miles around longed to win her hand.
But though she was a picture—the loveliest you've seen—
Sarah had another side. She could be *really* mean!

She wouldn't even let her friends touch her things, you see.
"Hands off my pretty toys," she'd shout. "They all belong to me!
Leave my precious jewels alone, and *please* don't touch my dress!
You'll only get it dirty, and make a horrid mess!"

Her friends grew quickly quite fed up: "Just keep your silly stuff.
We don't want to play with you. This time we've had enough!"
"How dare they speak to me like that!" cried Sarah in surprise.
She ran off to the woods to sulk, tears filling up her eyes.

Then Sarah heard a gentle voice. "There is no need to cry!
Every problem can be solved," said thoughtful Sir MacEye.
"Though your eyes shine like stars, and though you may be fair...
A kindly heart means so much more, so why not try to share?"

Sarah listened to his words. "How wise you are," she said.
"I don't need so many things! I'll share them out instead.
For though I love pretty things and clothes that make me fairer,
I'd rather share with my friends, and just be plain old Sarah!"

Snow White

One day, a queen gave birth to a beautiful little girl, who had skin as white as snow, cheeks as red as blood, and hair as black as ebony wood. She was called Snow White.

Sadly, the queen soon died. The king married again, and the new queen was beautiful but vain. Every day she stood before her magic mirror and asked: "Mirror, mirror, on the wall, who is the fairest one of all?"

The mirror always said: "You, oh Queen, are fairest of all!"

But little Snow White grew more and more lovely. At last the day came when the queen's magic mirror replied: "You, oh Queen, are fair, it's true. But Snow White is fairer than you!"

The queen was very angry. She summoned her huntsman.

"Take Snow White into the forest and kill her," said the wicked queen. "Bring me her heart in this chest."

So the huntsman took Snow White deep into the forest. But when he looked at Snow White he could not hurt her.

The huntsman killed a wild pig, put its heart in the chest, and returned to the castle. The wicked queen was pleased, for she was sure that Snow White was dead.

Lost and alone, Snow White stumbled through the dark forest until she came to a little cottage. She knocked at the door, but there was no answer. The door was unlocked, so she walked in.

Inside, she saw a little table with seven little plates of food. Snow White was hungry and ate some of the food.

Soon, Snow White felt sleepy. She found seven cozy little beds. She lay down on one of them and fell fast asleep.

The cottage belonged to seven dwarfs who worked in the gold mines. When they returned home that night, they found Snow White. She told them her story. They felt sorry for her.

"If you cook and clean for us," they said, "you can stay here and we will look after you." So Snow White decided to stay.

At the castle, the wicked queen was looking in her magic mirror. This time the mirror said: "Snow White is as lovely as she is good. She lives with the dwarfs, deep in the wood!"

The queen was furious. She decided to kill Snow White herself. She made a magic potion and used it to poison a pretty hair comb. Then she set out for the dwarfs' cottage dressed as a poor peasant woman.

"Pretty combs to buy!" she cried.

Snow White went outside. The witch offered to comb Snow White's hair. When the poisoned comb touched Snow White's beautiful black hair, she fell to the floor as if she were dead.

That night when the dwarfs came home, they found Snow White lying in the cottage garden.

At first they were in despair, but then one of them noticed the comb. Very gently, the eldest dwarf took the comb out of Snow White's hair. Soon, her pale cheeks grew rosy again.

The next morning, when the dwarfs left for the mines, they made sure Snow White locked the door and they kept the key.

This time, when the queen's magic mirror told her that Snow White was still alive, she roared with fury.

The wicked queen made a magic potion. With the potion she poisoned one half of a rosy apple. Then she set off to the dwarfs' cottage dressed as an apple-seller.

"Sweet, rosy apples to buy!" she called outside the window. But Snow White remembered the dwarfs' warning.

"I cannot let you in and I cannot come out," she said.

"Where is the harm in a sweet, rosy apple?" asked the apple seller. "Look, I will take a bite from this side. It is so sweet and juicy! Taste it for yourself."

Snow White took the poisoned apple. The moment she bit the poisoned apple, she fell down, lifeless.

When the dwarfs found Snow White lying on the floor again, they did everything they could to try to wake her. But she was still and cold.

The dwarfs made a beautiful glass coffin for Snow White. They set it among the flowers in their garden.

One day, a prince came riding through the forest. When he saw Snow White, he instantly fell in love with her. He begged the dwarfs to let him take the casket to his palace.

When the dwarfs lifted the casket, they stumbled. Suddenly a piece of poisoned apple fell from Snow White's mouth and her eyes opened. Snow White was alive!

Of course, the moment Snow White set eyes on the prince, she fell in love with him. When he asked Snow White to marry him, she happily agreed.

The next time the wicked queen looked into her magic mirror, it said: "You, oh Queen, are fair, it is true. But there is one still fairer than you. The bride that the prince will marry tonight is none other than the lovely Snow White!"

The wicked queen was so enraged that she fell down dead. And Snow White had nothing to fear ever again.

Princess Sleepyhead

Good night, Princess Sleepyhead!
It's time to climb the stairs to bed.
Tidy up. There's such a mess!
Neatly hang your pretty dress.

Brush your teeth. Make sure they're clean.
Brush up and down until they gleam!
Put your jewels in their box.
Brush your long and silky locks.

Snuggle down, switch on your light.
It shines just like the stars at night.
Sleep tight beneath its cozy beams—
Good night, Princess. Have sweet dreams!

Mermaid Princess Jade

Princess Jade wasn't just a mermaid princess. She was beautiful, too. And she knew it! She was the vainest mermaid in the sea.

One day the mermaids were all talking about the wreck of a pirate ship. On board was a treasure chest full of jewels. "But no one dares take the jewels," said the mermaids, "because the ship is cursed!"

"I'm going to find that pirate ship," Jade thought. "Just imagine how beautiful I will look wearing all those jewels!"

Jade swam to a part of the ocean she had never been to before. She swam down and down until she found the wreck. Jade swam inside and found the treasure chest.

She lifted out a necklace and put it around her neck. It was beautiful! But suddenly the necklace turned to stone around her neck. It was the ship's curse! Jade tried to swim, but the necklace was so heavy she couldn't move.

"Help!" Jade cried. "Help! Help!"

Jade's friend Gentle the giant turtle had followed her down to the shipwreck. He heard her and swam to the porthole.

"Help me, Gentle," cried Jade when she saw him.

Gentle's powerful flippers broke the necklace and freed Jade.

Once she was safely home, Jade told the other mermaids that she had learned her lesson. "I'll never be vain again!"

Cinderella

Once upon a time there was a pretty young girl who lived with her father, stepmother, and two stepsisters. The stepmother was unkind, and the stepsisters were mean.

Every day, the girl got up at dawn to cook and clean and wash and sew for her stepmother and stepsisters. Every night, the stepmother told the girl to sleep beside the fire. Soon the girl's clothes and hair were so gray with ash and cinders that everyone called her Cinderella.

One morning, a special invitation arrived. All the young women in the kingdom were invited to a ball at the royal palace so that the young prince could choose a bride.

The two stepsisters were very excited and ordered Cinderella around as she helped them get ready for the ball.

Cinderella sighed. She wished she could go with them.

As an elegant carriage took her stepsisters to the ball, Cinderella sat beside the hearth and wept.

"I wish I could go to the ball," she cried.

Suddenly, a strange light filled the room.

Cinderella looked up. A silvery glow surrounded a kind-looking woman with a glittering wand.

"Who are you?" asked Cinderella, blinking in wonder.

"I am your fairy godmother," the woman replied. "I have come to help you go to the ball."

"But how?" asked Cinderella.

"Find me a big pumpkin, six white mice, six frogs, and a rat," said the fairy godmother.

Cinderella found everything as quickly as she could.

The fairy godmother tapped the pumpkin with her wand. The pumpkin changed into a magnificent golden coach.

Next, the fairy godmother waved her wand over the six white mice. The six mice became six prancing horses.

The fairy godmother gently tapped her wand, and the six frogs changed into handsome footmen. One more tap, and the rat became a smart coachman.

With one last gentle tap of the wand, Cinderella's dusty dress became a shimmering ball gown. On her feet were two sparkling glass slippers.

"Now," said the fairy godmother, "you are ready for the ball. But at the stroke of midnight the magic will end, and everything will change back to what it was."

Cinderella promised to be home before midnight.

When Cinderella arrived at the palace, everyone turned to look at her. No one knew who Cinderella was. Even her own stepsisters didn't recognize her.

The prince thought that she was the loveliest, most enchanting girl he had ever seen. He danced only with her.

As Cinderella whirled around the room in his arms, she felt so happy that she forgot her fairy godmother's warning.

Suddenly, she heard the clock chime… twelve times!

"I must go!" cried Cinderella. And before the prince could stop her, she ran from the ballroom and out of the palace.

"Wait!" cried the prince, dashing after her. But by the time he reached the palace steps, all he could see was a ragged kitchen maid hurrying toward the palace gates.

Then he saw something twinkling on the steps—a single glass slipper. The prince picked it up.

"I will marry the woman whose foot fits this glass slipper," he declared. "I will search the kingdom until I find her."

The next day, the prince began going from house to house, looking for his true love. Every young woman in the kingdom tried on the glass slipper, but it didn't fit anyone.

At last the prince came to Cinderella's house. Her stepsisters were waiting to try on the slipper.

The first stepsister pushed and squeezed, but she could barely get her fat toes into the tiny slipper.

The second stepsister also tried to cram her foot into the shoe. But it was no use.

The prince was turning to leave when a soft voice asked, "May I try the slipper, please?"

As Cinderella stepped forward to try on the slipper, her stepsisters began to laugh.

"Get back to the kitchen where you belong!" ordered her stepmother.

"Everyone should have a chance," said the prince, "even a kitchen maid."

Cinderella sat down and took off her rough wooden clogs. The prince held out the sparkling slipper. And suddenly...

"Oh!" gasped her stepsisters.

Of course, Cinderella's dainty foot fitted into the slipper perfectly.

As her stepsisters gazed in amazement, the prince joyfully took Cinderella in his arms.

Her stepsisters and stepmother were still trembling with shock as they watched Cinderella ride off to the palace in the prince's own carriage.

Cinderella and the prince were soon married, and lived happily ever after.

The Enchanted Garden

Princess Sylvie loved to walk through the meadows to look at the flowers.

One day she found an overgrown path in her favorite meadow. She asked a woman where the path led.

"To the garden of the enchantress!" said the woman. "You can go and look, but they say that whatever you do, don't pick the flowers."

Princess Sylvie followed the path until she came to a cottage with the prettiest garden she had ever seen, filled with flowers of every color and perfume.

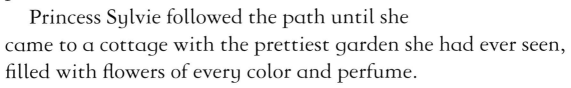

Princess Sylvie went back to the garden every day. Soon she forgot all about the enchantress—and one day, she picked a rose from the garden and took it back to the castle. As she put it in water, Princess Sylvie suddenly remembered the warning!

But months passed and nothing happened. The rose stayed as fresh as the day it was picked. Forgetting her fears, Princess Sylvie went back to the enchanted garden.

When she saw the garden, Princess Sylvie wanted to cry. The grass was brown. All the flowers had withered.

Then she heard someone weeping. Inside the cottage the enchantress was sitting by the fire, crying. She was old and bent. Princess Sylvie was afraid, but she felt sorry for her.

"What happened to your lovely garden?" Princess Sylvie asked.

"Someone picked a rose from it!" said the enchantress. "The garden is under a spell: the picked flower will live forever, but the rest of the flowers must die! And when the rose was picked, my magic was lost, too, and I too am beginning to wither and die!"

"What can I do?" asked Princess Sylvie, heartbroken.

"Only a princess can help," she replied. "She must bring me six sacks of stinging nettles! And no princess would do that!"

Princess Sylvie gathered six sacks of nettles, not caring that they stung her, and took them back to the enchantress.

The enchantress said, "But the nettles must be picked by a princess."

"I am a princess," said Princess Sylvie.

The enchantress made a magic potion with the nettles and drank it. Instantly, the garden became beautiful again—and Princess Sylvie gasped! Gone was the bent old lady. In her place was a beautiful young woman.

"My garden is restored," smiled the enchantress, "and so am I!"

And so the enchantress and the princess became dear friends and shared the enchanted garden.

Jolly Princess Polly

Polly was a funny kind of princess, it was thought.
She didn't always act the way a royal princess ought.
For everywhere that Polly went and every time she spoke,
She really couldn't help herself—*out* would pop a joke!

She snickered at royal functions, and laughed aloud at school.
She giggled in the library and broke the silence rule!
Though Polly was a lot of fun, and made her best friends smile,
She did get quite annoying—laughing all the while!

"If only Polly made less noise, and played more quietly,
Instead of laughing fit to burst!" complained her family.
Then one day disaster struck. Poor Polly lost her kitty.
She couldn't even raise a smile! It really was a pity.

"We wish that you would laugh again," said her friends that night.
"Without your laughter and your jokes, the palace isn't right!
If only we could find poor Fluff and make you smile again.
If we lose your happy face, it just won't be the same!"

All at once Sir Dave appeared, in answer to their wish.
"I found this by the moat," he said, "watching all the fish!"
Princess Polly laughed out loud, to everyone's delight.
"You've found little Fluff!" she cried, kissing the blushing knight.

Now Polly's jolly once again, so if they're feeling sad,
Her friends just listen to her laugh. It always makes them glad!

The Princess and the Pea

A long time ago, in a land far away, there lived a king and queen who had just one son. The prince was grown up, and it was time for him to marry a princess.

"And she must be a real princess," the prince told the king and queen.

But there were no princesses in the land where he lived, so the king and queen arranged for the prince to travel to strange and distant lands to find a bride.

The prince traveled north through frozen lands, until he came to a castle where a princess lived.

This princess was tall and fair and very smart. But she was also vain and boastful.

"A real princess would not be boastful," thought the prince. So he traveled south through hot, sandy deserts, until he came

to a palace where a princess lived.

This princess was very beautiful but was also very proud.

"A real princess would not be so proud," thought the prince. And he traveled east through misty lands, until he came to a mansion where a princess lived.

This princess had a charming smile and a lovely voice—but she told the most shocking lies!

"A real princess would never tell lies," thought the prince, so he returned home from his travels, weary, sad, and lonely.

One evening, not long after the prince had come home, a terrible storm blew in from the west.

Suddenly there was a knock at the palace door! The king was so surprised that he went to answer it himself.

There, standing in the windy doorway, was the most bedraggled young woman the king had ever seen.

"Good evening, Your Majesty," she said to the king, curtsying politely. "I am a princess, and I need shelter for the night. May I please come in?"

"Of course," said the king. "We will gladly give you shelter for the night."

When the king told the prince that a princess had turned up at the door, the prince was very eager to meet her. But the queen told him he would have to wait.

"The princess said that she couldn't possibly meet you wet and bedraggled," the queen explained. "She has gone to have a bath and change into some dry clothes."

"That's a good sign," said the prince. "But how can we be

certain that she is a real princess?"

"I have an idea," said his mother. "Leave everything to me."

A short while later, the princess arrived in the main hall dressed in the queen's clothes. Her hair shone, her cheeks were rosy, and her eyes sparkled merrily to match her smile.

The prince and princess sat beside the fire and talked for hours. The prince was enchanted—but he still wasn't sure that the princess was a real princess.

Meanwhile, the queen went to the best guest bedroom carrying a single tiny dried pea.

In the bedroom, she put the pea under the mattress. Then she asked a servant to bring another mattress to put on top of the first, and then another mattress, and another… until there were *twenty* mattresses on the bed!

Then the queen told the servant to put twenty soft, cozy quilts on top of the mattresses, and she had a ladder brought for the princess.

The princess was surprised when the queen brought her to the bedroom with its towering bed and ladder. But she didn't protest or complain. She thanked the queen and wished her good night.

The princess climbed the ladder to the very top of the bed. Sighing contentedly, she settled down to sleep. But the princess did not sleep a wink. She tossed and turned all night.

By morning, the princess felt tired and weary. When she came down to breakfast, the prince, the king, and the queen greeted her eagerly.

"Did you sleep well?" asked the queen.

"I'm afraid not," sighed the princess. "There was something small and hard in the bed, and no matter which way I turned, I still felt it. I'm dreadfully tired, for I hardly slept at all."

"I'm so sorry," said the queen. "But I'm delighted, too! For this proves that you are indeed a real princess! Only a real princess would feel a tiny pea under twenty mattresses and twenty quilts!"

The prince was overjoyed, for he had already fallen in love with the princess—and she had fallen in love with him. And so they were married.

And what happened to the pea? It was put on a velvet cushion in a glass case, and sent to the museum, where it is still on display today!

The Magical Locket

It was Princess Crystal's birthday, and her father, the king, had given her a magical locket.

"But it will only work if you say the magic rhyme," the king said.

"Magical locket, please listen well,
Help my friend with a kindly spell."

No one knew that, far away in her tower, the wicked witch was watching Princess Crystal's birthday in her crystal ball. When she saw the locket, the witch wanted it for herself.

The next day, Princess Crystal went riding. She didn't see the witch hiding behind a tree. As Princess Crystal trotted by, the wicked witch cast an evil spell. Princess Crystal's horse reared up and threw her to the ground.

As quick as a flash, the wicked witch threw a net over Princess Crystal and carried her away.

"Now the locket's mine!" she cried.

Soon they arrived at the witch's tower. A fierce dragon guarded it.

"Don't try to escape," said the witch, "or Horace the dragon will eat you up!"

At the top of the tower, the witch freed Princess Crystal. "Now give me your locket, and tell me the magic rhyme to go with it," she said.

"I won't give it to you," said Princess Crystal bravely.

"Then you can stay here until you do!" shouted the witch. She stormed out of the room, locking the door behind her.

Princess Crystal felt so alone. She leaned out of the window and began to cry. Her tears fell on Horace the dragon below.

"You're making me all wet," he said grumpily, flying up to her. "I'm not crying, even though my wing's broken and really hurts."

Princess Crystal felt sorry for the dragon. "Maybe I can help you," she said. She closed her eyes, held the locket and said the magic rhyme. Then Princess Crystal opened her eyes, and saw that Horace's wing had healed.

"Oh, thank you," he said happily. "My wing is healed, and I don't feel grumpy anymore. But what can I do to return your kindness?"

"Help me escape!" said Princess Crystal. She climbed out of the window and onto Horace's back. He flew her back to the palace. Princess Crystal never saw the wicked witch again.